The Sonic Life of a Giant Tortoise:

Youth is Not the Only Thing That's Sonic

Toshiki Okada

Translated by
Aya Ogawa

A SAMUEL FRENCH ACTING EDITION

SAMUEL FRENCH

FOUNDED 1830

SAMUELFRENCH.COM
SAMUELFRENCH-LONDON.CO.UK

FOR PRODUCTION ENQUIRIES

UNITED STATES AND CANADA
Info@SamuelFrench.com
1-866-598-8449

UNITED KINGDOM AND EUROPE
Plays@SamuelFrench-London.co.uk
020-7255-4302

Each title is subject to availability from Samuel French, depending upon country of performance. Please be aware that *THE SONIC LIFE OF A GIANT TORTOISE* may not be licensed by Samuel French in your territory. Professional and amateur producers should contact the nearest Samuel French office or licensing partner to verify availability.

MUSIC USE NOTE

Licensees are solely responsible for obtaining formal written permission from copyright owners to use copyrighted music in the performance of this play and are strongly cautioned to do so. If no such permission is obtained by the licensee, then the licensee must use only original music that the licensee owns and controls. Licensees are solely responsible and liable for all music clearances and shall indemnify the copyright owners of the play(s) and their licensing agent, Samuel French, against any costs, expenses, losses and liabilities arising from the use of music by licensees. Please contact the appropriate music licensing authority in your territory for the rights to any incidental music.

IMPORTANT BILLING AND CREDIT REQUIREMENTS

If you have obtained performance rights to this title, please refer to your licensing agreement for important billing and credit requirements.

THE SONIC LIFE OF A GIANT TORTOISE was first produced by The Play Company in New York City on May 24, 2014. The performance was directed by Dan Rothenberg, with sets by Mimi Lien, costumes by Jon Carter, lights by Jiyoun Chang, sound by Mikhail Fiksel, and choreography by David Brick. The Production Manager was Ian Guzzone and the Production Stage Manager was E Sara Barnes. The cast was as follows:

ACTOR 1	Dan Kublick
ACTOR 2	Jason Quarles
ACTOR 3	Moses Villarama
ACTRESS 1	Rachel Christopher
ACTRESS 2	Susannah Flood

CHARACTERS

ACTOR 1

ACTOR 2

ACTOR 3

ACTRESS 1

ACTRESS 2

PLAYWRIGHT'S NOTE

Text in parentheses indicates a character amending what he or she said previously.

1

ACTOR 1. What I'm about to say is something I've thought about in my head, in fact something I've never revealed to anyone else before. In other words, it is a kind of secret, so no one else besides me, not a single person, knows that I've kept the kind of thing I'm about to say inside my head. I'm going to tell you what kind of secret it is.

I really hope that my way of life improves compared to the way it is now. When I say that I hope it improves, I mean that I want to live more fully than I do now.

Whoah, but that kind of thing is, that I want to live more fully, it's just too, you know, or like, that may be something you think, but to actually say it out loud, even if you are thinking it, it's something you shouldn't articulate, so I keep it a secret.

But to be honest, I have been feeling, especially these days, that perhaps what I said just now, is really not something that I have to keep a secret inside my head at all, and it's actually fine for it to be out in the open, and in fact it's actually better that it is, or like it ought to be out in the open. To keep it unspoken as I have up until now might be, emotionally and psychologically speaking, unhealthy. So if I were to take a stand and say it out loud, clearly and honestly, maybe my current situation will take a turn for the better. I have been having these thoughts, these days especially, a little bit more frequently. There's a battle between saying things like that out loud, like "for people to know that, oh, is that what's on your mind, is, you know, a bit much" and the "but you should stop saying that because it's better to take a stand and tell the truth, just do it" and recently, the "it's better to just do it" side has been winning.

That's why, the secret that I am trying to tell right now, is something that is a secret I've kept from everyone up until now, but the time for it to be kept a secret may be coming to an end, because I may be bringing it to an end.

2

ACTRESS 1. The rest of my life, which, let's say I live to the average life expectancy for a Japanese person, and the Japanese have a pretty long life expectancy compared to the rest of the world, they say it's pretty high up there, so that means I have another forty, fifty, sixty years to go, let's say, and even if I do, that time between now and then will be a blink of an eye when it actually goes by... These are the vague thoughts that belong to a certain man. And that man is me.

Right, I think that, according to my suppositions, my life will probably come to an end with incredible speed.

What I'm about to tell you is a story about me. What I'm doing right now actually, despite what it looks like, is having a dream, and by dream, I mean the kind you have while you're sleeping, although there are some dreams you have while you are awake, but that is not the kind of dream I'm having right now.

ACTOR 2. (And when I said dreams you have while you are awake, I wasn't referring to daydreams but normal hopes you have for your real life, like, "oh I wish such and such will happen in the near future," that's what I meant by dreams.)

ACTRESS 1. Right, I am now having a dream. So despite what it looks like, I actually have my eyes closed.

Where I have my eyes closed, or like where I am sleeping now is the apartment I live in. It's now five or six o'clock in the morning. I will wake up in a little while. When my alarm goes off, I will hit the snooze button once or twice, but I will give up the third time it goes off. But right now I am still dreaming.

If I were to describe the kind of dream I am having right now, actually, it would fall into the category of really good dreams. The reason why it is really good is because it is one of those bittersweet dreams. If my dreams were organized on shelves according to genre, this dream would be kept on the shelf reserved for dreams that cause heartache. I am having that kind of dream right now.

It's a bittersweet dream because in the dream I'm having now, I had a girlfriend. (By the way I have a girlfriend in real life, not just in my dreams.) Right, in the dream I'm having right now, I had a girlfriend, but actually, my girlfriend had actually died, in the past, but because it's a dream, I don't have a clear sense of whether it was a few years ago, a few months ago, or a few days ago. I'm not sure what the cause of her death is, in my dream, but anyway this is the backstory to the dream I'm having now.

My girlfriend has died and is no longer here, and will never return – even though it's just something that's in my dream, I still feel heartache over it. Time after time, or perhaps, sometimes, or perhaps, once in a while, the frequency changes with the situation but, I remember her. And every time I think of her, I experience that bittersweet feeling. In my dream.

If I had to explain what that bittersweet feeling felt like to someone who didn't know what that felt like, although I don't think such a person actually exists, but say for sake of argument I had to explain it to them, I would say that when you experience that feeling, what happens to you physically, for example, is something like this: for example, I would say it feels like something is pushing back up towards my solar plexus from below, and it pushes all the way up towards the base of my nose, and then it very subtly taps into my tear ducts. Or, if I were to think of another way to describe it, it's like this: the sensation you feel in your belly when you're really hungry, I think it would be accurate to say that it's very similar to that sensation, it's like there's a hole in your body, or like a hollow, and around that hollow, I mean the area of your body around that hollow, that whole area feels like it's trying to fill that vacuum. But, and this is obvious of course, there's no way for your body to do that, so you remain in that state, and you experience this not in your belly, but slightly above, around where your stomach is, and around your chest, that's what that bittersweet feeling feels like in your body. This might have been a confusing analogy but.

I am experiencing this bittersweet sensation in the dream I am having right now, and I think that it feels really good. I may be saying this off-hand without a really deep understanding of what it means to live, but to be able to feel this emotion makes me feel really alive, and I think to have that actual experience just feels really good. In my dream I am thinking, I must live feeling this continual wistfulness from here on out, for the entire rest of my life, for the next forty, fifty, sixty years until I die. And if that is so, I have a feeling, I mean it's just speculation but, I will have lived that lifetime with a strong sense of having really lived. Once I awake, I will have no ability to follow what would have happened to my dreaming self but, I am watching my dream, imagining that my dreaming self will continue to live to the end of his life like this, and thinking how wonderful that is and how envious I am

OK so, everything I've said up to now has been about the dream I'm having now. But from here on, I will be talking not about my dreams, but me in real life. In my real life, as I mentioned earlier, I have a girlfriend. And that girlfriend of mine in my real life, unlike the one in my dream, is not dead, and in reality is alive. Since she is alive, she does all sorts of things. For example, she comes to my apartment. I have in my room, a small table, which was purchased for the purpose of her occasional visits. I also have two chairs. This chair is hers. The other day, she was saying that she wanted to take a trip overseas.

3

ACTRESS 1. I want to travel.

ACTOR 2. Is that so?

ACTRESS 1. What do you mean "Is that so?" You ought to know.

ACTOR 2. You say that you want to travel pretty regularly.

ACTRESS 1. If I were to travel, I don't really care where, as long as I'm able to go somewhere.

ACTOR 2. I have no interest in travel. I can't imagine that my feelings about it will change.

ACTRESS 1. I said that I don't care where, but that's not exactly true, the truth is that, if it were possible, I would of course love to visit a foreign country, but basically, I don't have a place in mind that I've dreamt about that I want to visit.

I wish that we both had this shared interest in traveling.

ACTRESS 2. Actually, I haven't woken up yet from the dream I was telling you about. My alarm clock hasn't gone off yet.

ACTOR 2. Isn't traveling a hassle?

ACTRESS 1. If we were to take a trip, (even domestically), when would we be able to go?

ACTOR 2. When I went to Paris a while back, I went to the Eiffel Tower and, the Eiffel Tower was fine and all, but around the Eiffel Tower, there were all of these like vendors, and they were all clearly from the looks of them, like immigrant types, and they were all selling these cheap-looking like toys, or miniatures this size of the Eiffel Tower, with these blinking lights on them, and everyone was selling the same Eiffel Tower everywhere.

ACTRESS 1. I want to go to Paris.

ACTRESS 2. I am not only having this dream, but I'm also thinking about my real life, sort of juxtaposed with the dream. By real life, I specifically mean my real life girlfriend.

ACTOR 2. What do you find so fun about traveling?

ACTRESS 1. All of it.

ACTOR 2. Is it because you have this feeling like "I want to see the whole world!" that you want to travel?

Most of the human beings on Earth spend their entire lives without ever traveling far.

ACTRESS 1. Yeah. Why are you saying it like that?

ACTOR 2. What I think is important is what can I do to get to a place where you don't think that you want to travel anymore. I'll think about that.

ACTRESS 2. To be perfectly honest about how I feel about my real life girlfriend, what I think about is, I wish that my living real life girlfriend were just like my girlfriend in my dream, dead.

…I mean, isn't that outrageous?

ACTRESS 1. I am debating whether or not I should come out and say that it's naïve to think that way about the Eiffel Tower.

ACTOR 2. There's a chance that she is thinking, "What a hypocrite."

There's something I'd like to ask. How can one escape from hypocrisy? How?

To say that "all" of traveling is fun, is definitely a lie.

ACTRESS 1. I don't think that's a "lie."

ACTOR 2. Are there really no elements of travel that are not enjoyable, not even one?

ACTRESS 1. Why do I have to frantically search to see whether there is or not?

I just want to travel.

ACTRESS 2. I think that what I said earlier may invite some gross misunderstandings, in the way that I expressed what I did, so allow me to append what I said so that there aren't any misunderstandings. I didn't mean, by what I said earlier, that I want my living girlfriend to die. It's just that sometimes I might think that things might be better if my girlfriend were someone who was no longer alive, that's all. For example, it would make me feel much more nostalgic for her. Or in other words, ummm, this is really awkward but, I am not wishing that my living girlfriend would die, but what I am thinking is that, (huh?) if I had to put it into words, I think that the bottom line would be this: Do I think that it would be nice to have someone who has died as a girlfriend?

What if my reality were that my girlfriend had died. She's gone. Let's just say that that is my reality. If that were the case, for example, I think that there's a good chance that the me who is living in that reality would be living a better life than me who's living in this day-to-day now. By better life I mean, that the amount of emotion I would experience, like wistfulness for example, would be much greater for me in that reality than it is for me now, every day.

If I were living in that reality, for example, I would look at this chair here, and once in a while, or sometimes, or time after time I would recall the times I spent with her, what I did with her, her face, her expressions, her voice, the things she said. This chair would become imbued with meaning everyday from that wistfulness. It would be, what, somehow more profound than my life now, to spend my life with such objects and to be offered those feeling of caring for her – I imagine that that would feel really nice.

But in reality, actually, my girlfriend is not dead, she's alive, like a normal person, and she does and talks about a lot of different things and that's not in the past tense, she does these things now, in the present tense.

4

ACTOR 1. "I live in Japan, in Tokyo, and I really like Tokyo. What I especially like about Tokyo is that the energy of the city is always kind of swirling, everywhere you go there are a lot of people, and heat, not just people but cars, information, the hustle and bustle, there's like a WOW energy, a feeling that so many different things are thrown together in a stew, there's like a vibration that naturally wells up when you're here, this incredible amount of energy, creating this constant chaos of different elements – that's what I love about Tokyo."

OK so, that was a total lie, that was not me speaking from the heart but just something I made up on the spot, because honestly, I don't think that Tokyo is the kind of city that emanates this power or energy or vibration at all. But I think that there are a lot of people in the world who say that they "feel that kind of thing from Tokyo." But I don't feel that at all. Of course I might be in the minority.

"The thing I find most exciting about Tokyo, living here, is that on the one hand, there's the very traditional culture, and on the other hand there's the high tech aspect, and both of these co-exist very naturally. But when you really think about it, the fact that both of these extremes are able to co-exist as if it were normal is actually a remarkable thing, I think, and depending on how you look at it, it's pretty cool, and that's what I like about Tokyo, and it makes me feel good about living in a city like this."

That was a lie too. I couldn't get behind those words either, I was kind of just letting myself talk by taking an averaged out sampling of the answers that people like Hollywood stars or directors for movie promos or like musicians who are touring to the Tokyo Dome or the Budokan have as canned answers for interviews when they're asked what they think of Tokyo.

(Those kinds of stars and stuff really have it rough, because they have to answer those questions with a straight face, questions that really seem totally idiotic, like why bother asking them, and are so clichéd. Of course those guys are making crazy bank and staying in hotel suites, so I guess on one hand they have to do as much.)

5

ACTOR 2. In general, dying is normally considered something to be afraid of, and if someone is not afraid to die, that person is considered to be somewhat special. By special, I mean, for example, someone who has trained as an ascetic and reached enlightenment, that kind of special. On the other hand, special could also mean someone who's like I don't care what happens to my life, I'm going to kill myself.

However, if I were to say whether I am afraid of dying, I'd say that I'm not particularly afraid at all. But I shouldn't be considered a special kind of person. I think I am a regular person. Or maybe I've reached enlightenment? Do I look like an enlightened person? Or maybe I am actually suicidal? Do I look like someone who is suicidal?

ACTRESS 1. I don't understand why we have to spend time thinking about what we could do to be able to spend our daily life without ever thinking that we want to travel.

ACTOR 2. We want to live a fulfilling life. The day-to-day plays an important part in that. In fact the day-to-day is much more important that taking a trip somewhere.

ACTRESS 1. If you're trying to impose the logic that "Every day would be more fun if we could spend our days as if we were traveling," I think that's mistaken.

I can't understand what's so wrong for me to think very simply that I want to travel. I can't change the way I think, is it because I'm stupid?

"The day-to-day is important," what, is that some kind of philosophy? I know it's wrong for me to say this but honestly, I don't like it. Or like it's a lot of pressure. I want to travel.

ACTOR 2. Somehow we often arrive at this tense impasse, when we're in the house together for extended periods of time.

We want to live a fulfilling life.

ACTRESS 1. I think I could if I could travel.

I want to travel.

ACTOR 3. Right now, I have one idea, besides traveling, that might be a solution to this tension, and I'm just hesitating to say it out loud, but the idea is this, "I, I think that in order for us not to get tense with each other, we should make an effort to be more conscious about or think more about all the different events and news that are going on in the world. I think that that would be in our best interest. We should watch the news and stuff more often and think about these things not like they're someone else's problems, but that they are our problems, personally, so even if we end up stressed out like this, there might be a way for us to break ourselves out of it" so. But in reality I never shared this with her, and instead I say them to the girlfriend in my dreams, who is already dead. Then, I imagine, if it were my girlfriend from my dream, I think that maybe she would say something like, "Suppose, there is one way that I feel the connection I have with the world which is that, if I were, for example, like this, lying around, or leaning up against a wall sitting on the floor, sometimes I can sense myself and sense the Earth turning, both its rotation and its orbital motion, and I can feel that I am turning with the Earth, of course that's just my imagination. There's no actual way I could sense that, but sometimes there are moments where I feel like I can sense that motion, and when that happens, I think to myself, oh, the world and I are moving together at the Earth's pace right now."

(Um, I imagine that everyone has done this at least once but, for example when you have a headache or when you have a toothache, you pinch the back of your hand or your cheek to supercede the pain you already feel, and it makes you forget the pain of your head or tooth, I mean even if you've never actually tried that I think that we've all at least thought about it as an idea, so basically what I'm doing here is fundamentally the same thing, if I say so... But as a practical matter, everyone uses techniques like this to break out of stressful situations, of course.)

6

ACTOR 2. What I'm really doing right now, despite what it looks like, is riding on the subway. I'm heading to my job. (But actually we could do the part where I'm already at my job, and looking at my computer screen, but...hmmm, but no I'll do the subway bit.)

I am sitting on the subway seat, but I'm not really aware of it. Because I'm in a very light sleep, or like I'm in between sleep and a kind of spaced out thinking about something. The subway is very crowded, as usual it's full of people heading to work.

Ordinarily one would assume that I would eventually wake up, and it would happen as my neck would jerk forward. In fact that would be what would wake me up.

But let's not think about the ordinary, let's think about what would happen if we did not assume the ordinary. For example: I don't wake up. I think that possibility seems more interesting, so let's think further about that. In that case, if I don't wake up, let's say that I don't ever wake up for the rest of my life. I imagine that I would just continue to ride on this subway, endlessly. Gradually I realize that this train is no longer making any stops. And somehow, I can tell that our course is now at a very slight slope going downhill. We are plunging deeper and deeper underground. It keeps going deeper, forever and ever, in other words this subway is not moving in the direction of my office anymore, in fact, in this situation I would never have to go to work again.

This subway will really keep running forever, (and in fact moving deeper underground), and I begin to gradually realize that it seems like I will most likely be ending my entire life in this subway. My life will probably be as long as the average life expectancy for a Japanese (although of course this is hypothetically speaking), but until my life ends I will remain in this subway, and the subway will keep running for that length of time, non-stop. I have to admit that imagining this is, just imagining it is…it's pretty out there, it's a pretty amazing scenario, it's wonderful, it's almost like a dream or like, it's a great image. I wish I could stay here forever. I feel like that would be just wonderful.

It's true, when I look back on it, my life was a pretty good life. If not a good life, a very comfortable life. People say that life is full of pitfalls, running into walls, and stuff like that but, in the end, I feel like I got away without those cruelties for the most part. As far as the rest of my life, I just have to keep riding this subway, so. So it will probably be fine. Essentially I had no pitfalls or walls to run into, and that is a very fine thing. I think maybe it's that, despite whatever we think about the human race, we actually have advanced. The fact that living has become consistently more comfortable. Of course there are things that have become more difficult, as a consequence. But as far as I'm concerned, all I have to do is keep riding this subway.

7

ACTOR 2. Ordinarily, if one were to imagine what would happen next in this extraordinary line of thought, I'd probably keep riding the subway and this story would just come to an end. But let's think about a different possible outcome. The train suddenly comes to a stop. And someone comes and wakes me up. We'll take it from there.

(**ACTRESS 2** *wakes up* **ACTRESS 1**.)

ACTOR 2. *(to* **ACTRESS 1***)* Ask her, "Where are we?"

ACTRESS 1. Where are we?

ACTRESS 2. Before we get to that, do you mind? Didn't you do a little something nice the other day?

ACTRESS 1. Me? A little something nice? What do you mean by a little something nice? Are you talking about sex?

ACTRESS 2. Oh, no.

ACTRESS 1. I haven't had sex recently.

ACTRESS 2. What I meant by a little something nice was a kind deed.

ACTRESS 1. A kind deed? Me? That I did? When could it have been?

ACTRESS 2. It was the other day, someone, a stranger was playing with a ball, kicking it around and he missed, and when that ball came rolling towards you, you picked it up and gave it back to him, didn't you?

ACTRESS 1. Did I do something like that? I don't remember.

Oh, wait I do remember. Oh, yes, yes, I did do something like that, now that you mention it, I remember now. I did do that.

Or like, I'm sorry, I totally remember doing that, but the fact that I remembered something like that seemed really small of me so I couldn't readily admit to it.

ACTRESS 2. *(pointing to a man)* When this man was kicking a ball around and it came rolling towards you, did you pick it up and give it back to him?

Yeah, so, can we say that you gave it back to him?

To tell you the truth, we've organized a little event or like a party to thank you and it's all set to go, the venue is very close by here, and in fact the dance floor is already jumping, so you're welcome to come dance and we have several DJs lined up for the night and we also have a band scheduled, of course we have some drinks and refreshments prepared as well, so if you wouldn't mind joining us, that would be great, but there's just one thing that concerns me, perhaps you don't really like, or aren't into that kind of thing?

ACTRESS 1. No.

ACTRESS 2. I understand. Then let's forget about that, since this is to express the thanks from the man whose ball you returned, let me ask you this, let me ask you what would you like? Instead of a big crazy party, what would you prefer?

ACTRESS 1. Me? Um, can it be anything at all?

ACTRESS 2. Yes.

ACTRESS 1. Then, I'd like to travel.

ACTRESS 2. I understand.

A trip, then, and do you have a destination in mind?

ACTRESS 1. I only have the vague idea that I'd love for it to be to a foreign country, but basically, it doesn't matter, I'd just like to go anywhere.

ACTRESS 2. I understand.

By the way, taking the subway here was itself a small trip I think, did this feel like you were taking a trip? Or not?

Oh, but you don't have to go out of your way to make this experience count towards your desire to travel.

ACTRESS 1. I came here on the subway just now but, I got on thinking I was heading towards work as usual, but the route changed from the middle, and when I realized that we were going a different way, at first I was like what should I do, and I panicked, thinking that I'd be in trouble if I just stayed on the train, but I also felt this, screw it, who cares what happens kind of attitude, both at the same time, kind of situation, you see.

ACTRESS 2. Yes.

ACTRESS 1. Um.

ACTRESS 2. Yes.

ACTRESS 1. The party? Is it OK for me to check it out?

ACTRESS 2. Would you like to go? Wonderful.

ACTRESS 1. Yes.

(She goes.)

8

ACTOR 2. So, next. I had never been to a place where there was a dance floor that glimmered with colorful lights, so this was my first time. But in the end I didn't really dance that much, I just watched other people dance. I think I was watching for less than an hour, but it was really fun, I mean for me it was all very refreshing so. A lot of people came up to me and talked to me. Of course it was a party thrown in my honor, so that was to be expected. I said a lot of people but it was about two people, maybe three. I hung out with some of those people in this lounge-type area, and we're going to do that part now.

ACTRESS 1. Looking back on it, I do feel like there was a part of me that might have been too cynical, I would say that's what I regret.

ACTOR 1. Really?

ACTRESS 1. Really.

ACTOR 1. Huh, can you give me an example?

ACTRESS 1. An example? OK for example, take a straight-up sentimental song, like a totally stereotypical song with a positive message in the lyrics, I think it would have been better if I were the type of person who could listen to a song like that without irony and be moved to tears by it. I've come this far in life without ever wanting to admit that I would like a song like that but, when I think about it now, I kind of feel like I could have used some of that inside me.

ACTOR 1. Really.

ACTRESS 1. Oh and also I wish I had had a friend from a foreign country. As long as I'm talking about what I wish had been different.

ACTOR 1. Really.

ACTRESS 1. I wouldn't go as far to say that I wish I had had a really close friend from another country, I didn't want one that badly. Just a casual acquaintance would have been fine, someone from a foreign country who loved Japan, or Tokyo and who would say stuff like, "This is what's so awesome about Tokyo!" and that would charm me, or like make me feel content in the knowledge that oh, there are people in the world who feel that way.

ACTOR 1. Yes that's nice.

ACTRESS 1. And ultimately I'd have the hope that they would make me like Tokyo and Japan too. You know how there are a lot of Japanese people who are overly critical of Tokyo and stuff?

ACTOR 1. Sure.

ACTRESS 1. Even though they live in Tokyo themselves. What do you think about people like that?

ACTOR 1. I hate them.

ACTRESS 1. Totally, right?

ACTOR 1. You're free to say bad things about whatever. But then, don't live here.

ACTRESS 1. Totally, right? So on the opposite end of the spectrum, I basically really love people who say they like Tokyo, and if this friend came to Tokyo and liked it, and was really glad that they came here, it would make me so happy, I'd feel like, thank you, so I had been thinking that it would be so nice to hear opinions like that regularly. I mean, you can't have enough opinions like that, right? That's why I thought it would be fun to have a friend from a foreign country. So I would say that that was another regret, if I'm talking about regrets.

ACTOR 1. Really.

But hey, this isn't like, you know, the afterlife or anything.

ACTRESS 1. Oh really?

ACTOR 1. Did you think you were dead?

ACTRESS 1. Yes.

ACTOR 1. Do you want to talk about something else? What's a good topic? *(to* **ACTOR 3***)* Talk about something.

ACTOR 3. Something? What do you like?

ACTRESS 1. What do I like? I like traveling. But it's not like I've traveled a lot, in fact, I haven't traveled much at all.

ACTOR 3. Then what are your dislikes?

ACTRESS 1. The day-to-day.

ACTOR 3. That was a quick response.

ACTRESS 1. Yes.

But the fact that I dislike the day-to-day is not quite, really it's not that I dislike it at all, but, hey what do you think about this? Do you think that daily life has to be fun or like necessarily has to be remarkable? Like isn't it better to have something enjoyable in normal life regularly, like one sparkly highlight of the day type thing? Or like, to put it another way, don't you think that there's a lot of pressure from the world that if you don't have something fun in daily life there's something wrong?

ACTOR 1. There totally is.

ACTRESS 1. What I dislike is that pressure, and if it weren't for that pressure, I probably wouldn't dislike the day-to-day itself at all.

ACTOR 1. Day-to-day, huh. In the end our greatest problem lies therein.

I think it's the same across the board for all humanity.

It's annoying.

ACTRESS 1. Oh you mean regular life?

ACTOR 1. Yeah. But do you know how to not make it annoying?

ACTRESS 1. Who me? I don't know.

ACTOR 1. I do.

In fact I have my own theory on the topic.

What it is is, if you take a look at all of the various problems in the world, there's the idea that all of the issues fundamentally originate in the home, in the living quarters, right?

ACTRESS 1. Yes.

ACTOR 1. We all put our roots down in our homes, and we all operate under the assumption that basically all of us will settle down in one place, that's how the world turns, in other words from a certain perspective I think you could say that every single issue that arises in the world has its origins in real estate.

ACTRESS 1. Yes.

ACTOR 1. Take daily life for example. I mean what is the day-to-day, in the end, if it isn't about settling down? There is a house and you settle there, in other words that is the point where what you call your daily life is born. So basically, let's throw out the idea of settling down. If we throw that concept out, then it will follow that daily routine will disappear. Don't settle down, don't put your roots down, don't have a regular address. Without a home, you have to keep moving from one place to another, it could be a hotel, or staying at a friend's house, I mean don't you think about that sometimes?

ACTRESS 1. Yes.

ACTOR 1. Everyone has the same idea. What a wonderful existence that would be, the idea and an admiration for that idea visits us from time to time.

ACTRESS 1. It does.

ACTOR 1. But practically speaking, how could you actually build a life like that now? When you start thinking about it, on the one hand, it doesn't go anywhere, so in that sense, the idea stops there, so, it's just an experiment in imagination, that's all.

So in that sense, I think that travel is a great realistic solution. Although I've never traveled anywhere myself.

Of course this is my own personal theory, and what I always say is, ultimately, the home should just vanish. What do you think?

Sometimes, after I've said something like what I've just said, there's some idiot who argues, "What? But even if we didn't have a home, we would still have daily life, right?" And he usually thinks he's doing me a favor by pointing that out, and I'm like what a fucking idiot, you just don't get it do you? To guys like that, I have no choice but to break it down point by point, yeah of course, we would have a daily life even without a home, but that kind of daily life is an entirely different kind of daily life than the day-to-day we've identified as being so problematic. In other words, of course daily routine exists outside of the problem at hand, a daily life that doesn't have the kind of problems that we're talking about, which means that that daily life isn't defined by the problems that we have with our current daily life, which means that we could essentially say that that is not daily life.

What do you think?

You think I'm crazy?

At the dawn of humanity, did you know this, there were no permanent settlements.

ACTRESS 1. Because as hunters we'd have to keep on the move?

ACTOR 1. Precisely.

So the question is, why did we begin to settle down, do you know?

ACTRESS 1. Isn't it because that was more comfortable?

ACTOR 1. You might think so, but that's not correct, in fact it's the opposite, it isn't more comfortable to stay in one place, do you know why?

I mean for example, if you settled down, you'd have to clean your home, right? Keep house? If you didn't have a home, all you'd have to do is just move to a different spot once the old spot is dirty. You don't have to build a toilet. That's much easier. You don't need such a tedious thing as a sewage system. Or a waste management system.

So why did we begin to settle down, can you guess?

ACTRESS 1. Because we started agriculture?

ACTOR 1. That's right. Actually, before agriculture, we started fishing. Yeah.

Do you know why fishing would necessitate settlement?

It's pretty simple, fishing instruments like boats and fishing nets are all big and heavy right? Not easy to transport. So basically if you're using them by the seashore, you want to just leave them by the seashore. But then you can't move around. But the tools for hunting, like spears and bows and traps are pretty light. Yeah. Do you know why we stopped hunting and started fishing?

Obviously it's because fish are delicious. That was a joke of course. Wasn't that funny? Fish are dumber than the animals that live on land, so they're easier to catch, for one. The thing about deer and boar is that they'll learn how to avoid traps and stuff, but fish, they never learn, so they can be caught in nets forever.

But as a result, humankind, as a result of settlement, has been burdened by daily life. We reap what we sow. It's too much of a consequence to pay. It's got to end.

So as a conclusion, we should not eat any more fish or vegetables ever again. From now on, everybody's got to live by eating only meat, and beyond that, nuts and berries from trees.

ACTRESS 1. But nowadays our meat comes from the cows and stuff raised on farms.

ACTOR 1. I know that, you idiot!

A mere ten thousand years ago, humankind had not settled down. And look at where we are now.

Take the U.S. dollar – it has completely finished playing its historic role as the key currency. And yet we still worship America, America, I mean if we keep depending on America, Japan is seriously going to reach its demise.

ACTRESS 1. Um.

ACTRESS 2. Yes.

ACTRESS 1. Can I get home from here?

ACTRESS 2. You can.

ACTRESS 1. Is it that way?

ACTRESS 2. Yes. Can you find you way?

ACTRESS 1. Yes.

ACTRESS 2. Are you gonna go home?

ACTRESS 1. I think so.

ACTRESS 2. I understand.

ACTRESS 1. But I really enjoyed this. I'm glad I came.

ACTOR 1. Wait a second. You've just been standing and watching this whole time, why don't you dance?

You want to travel, huh? Give me a fucking break.

Everything I said just now is written in this book.

Hey you could stay a little while longer!

(**ACTRESS 1** *leaves.*)

9

ACTOR 3. "The way you are living is a far cry from how humankind ought to be living." Make no mistake, even if there is nothing we can do to change it, I think that this is true of the way we are living our lives. I wouldn't be surprised if even worse things were said, something like, "You people are not living at all," and even then, there is a greater chance that we would have nothing to say for ourselves, the way we are living now.

No matter what anyone says, the fact is I already know that myself. And the fact is, I'm fine with the way we live.

On one level, there's nothing we can do about the fact that we are not living the way humankind ought to live. In fact, I think that in fact it's good that we're not, part of me is relieved. Because I don't think we could bear it, we aren't cut out for the way humankind ought to live.

That's all.

10

ACTOR 2. So, next. I returned. Then I went to my boyfriend's apartment. And to my surprise, he had aged incredibly, he was two hundred and fifty years old and had become bedridden. I stayed there for a while, taking care of him. But very soon, after about fifteen minutes or so, he breathed his last breath.

11

ACTRESS 1. What I am doing now is, riding the subway again. I'm riding thinking it would be awesome to be able to get back to that place before, but I understand somewhere inside me that, even if I stay on this train I'll never be able to make my way back there.

In the room earlier, I was looking for something like a letter that I thought I might find, which is something I imagined myself, and what I imagined the contents of that letter to be was something like, "I would like to be able to say that I have lived my life to the fullest, but in order to do that, if I continue to drag my feet for the remainder of the time I have, in other words, for the rest of my life until I die, the rest of my life will really come to an end in a blink of an eye, so I must hurry." But I didn't find any letter or anything like that.

I do know that it's true that our banal day-to-day existence is connected to something much bigger. I mean, putting aside the issue that it's difficult for me to really feel that that is true from the bottom of my heart, and to continuously believe in it, I do know it as a fact. It is really so difficult for me that it's almost beyond my imagination, so I tend to pretty pragmatically come around to thinking that maybe I don't have to make an effort to hold on to this belief, in fact I've probably already let the idea go. Does this mean that I have no gumption or strength? But am I the only one who lacks such strength? Are other people able to do it? Or is everybody unable to? If nobody can do it, then maybe it's not such a tragedy? Or does it mean that everybody altogether has failed? This may be something that I do in order to just protect myself but, when I start thinking about myself as a failure, I immediately think that it's got to be unhealthy for me to think of myself as a failure and that I should try to change the way I think, so in other words, this is what I think: the reason we lack the strength to hold on to that idea must mean that actually there is no need for us to hold on to it, so we don't have to try to hold on, so there's no reason to get depressed that we can't. For example, we can't fly through the sky like birds, but that's because there's no need for us to fly, it's totally fine that we can't fly – this is the same idea.

12

ACTOR 1. What I'm doing now is, despite what it looks like, I'm at my job, working on my computer at my desk, I'm in a staring match with the computer screen. In other words, everyone, you are positioned as if you are looking at me through my computer screen. I am working very diligently. At lunch time, I'm thinking I'll visit some travel sites and do some research about travel, but I am responsible so I don't do things like that during business hours, or like, this may be obvious but, this computer might be monitored by my company, so I can't really do stuff like that for fear of being caught.

Wait. Wait a second. Does that mean, if all of you are looking at me through my computer screen, are you perhaps actually my company? (What would that mean if you were my company? Would it be that you were the system administrators at my company?)

By the way, I am not aware of the fact that I am being watched through the computer screen. I mean, that's not something you'd ordinarily think, that you're being watched from a place like that? And if I were aware that I was being watched, I wouldn't be making a face like this, I would be wearing a much more serious expression like, "I am a very capable worker." I have this habit of whenever I'm working at the computer, or even when I'm spacing out, I let my mouth hang open, and it's a habit I've had since I was a child, and I haven't been able to get rid of it even as an adult. It's not such a good habit, I mean of course it doesn't look good, for one, and also when you keep your mouth open, the inside of your mouth gets really dry, and it makes me tend to catch colds easily.

> (**ACTRESS 1** *puts on an expression of "I am a very capable worker."*)

Oh, that's the expression, isn't it, "I am a very capable worker." I wonder why I suddenly made that face? That was a momentary mystery. Maybe I'll do it again.

(After a while she does it again.)

I did!

(ACTRESS 1 *smiles.)*

End